THE RED CAMP

DEBRA DIAZ

Arte Público Press
Houston, Texas
1996

This volume is made possible through grants from the National Endowment for the Arts (a federal agency), Andrew W. Mellon Foundation, and the Lila Wallace-Reader's Digest Fund.

Recovering the past, creating the future

Arte Público Press
University of Houston
Houston, Texas 77204-2090

Cover illustration and design by Kath Christensen

Diaz, Debra
    The red camp / by Debra Diaz.
       p.   cm.
    ISBN 1-55885-169-0 (trade paper : alk. paper)
    I. Title.
    PS3554.I258R4   1996
    813'.54—dc20   96-16936
                                              CIP

Para
Rosalie y Mario
and
Annette, Ramona, Sylvia and Lorraine

Contents

El Padre/The Father

La Madre/The Mother

Emily

Introduction

El Campo Colorado was a citrus worker camp
built in the early 1900's by a local growers' associa-
tion to house Mexican-American and Mexican immi-
grant workers in Orange County, California.
Conceived by the citrus growers under the pretense
of concern for decent migrant-worker housing, El
Campo Colorado was in reality constructed to pro-
vide the growers with the readily available and stable work force required for the rapidly expanding
southern California citrus industry.

The local growers gambled correctly in employ-
ing Latino workers, for unlike the previous Japan-
ese and before them Chinese workers, the majority
of the Mexicans and Mexican-Americans did not
pursue land ownership and therefore could not com-
pete with the growers in the citrus business. Latinos soon became the citrus "worker of choice" in the
region, and statewide as well.

Like most worker camps, El Campo Colorado
was calculatedly situated away from the main com-
munity. Located on a gently sloping, treeless plain
to the south of town, it was adjacent to the railroad
tracks and next to a small but growing barrio.

The individual camp houses, more like barracks
than homes, were narrow three-roomed units, with
a shared outdoor water pump and outhouse. The
Latino families made the most of what was available, and many grew small vegetable gardens and
raised chickens, ducks and goats.

The citrus boom of the forties created a steady
demand for laborers, which in turn drew workers'
relatives to the area. At times, the whole settlement
appeared to be related. Small businesses sprung up,
including three small grocery stores, two bars and a
pool hall. The camp served not only as a home, but
as an extended family for its people, and over the
years it developed a warm, cooperative and friendly
personality. From the teens through the 1950's, the
camp was, at its largest, home to approximately
seventy-five families.

The work camp was known by many names—El
Campo Colorado, el barrio, The Camp, and even
"Little Mexico"—by the growers and townspeople,
but the name favored by the camp children was the
"The Red Camp," nicknamed so because of the red-
wood used in the construction of the homes and
because of the red tar shingles that topped the roof
of each home.

By the 1950's, burgeoning suburbanization, the subsequent loss of agricultural land and the migration of Latinos to more secure and higher paying jobs outside of agriculture, caused the camp population to dwindle as the barrio population grew. In the early 1960's, with most of the fields and groves gone, the camp was razed to make room for a trailer park. The nearby barrio, however, inherited the camp name and continued to grow, exchanging its hardworking citrus pickers for hardworking blue-collar workers. Today the name El Campo Colorado remains, a reminder of sorts of the many hardships and the too few joys of the families who came before and of those who continue to follow.

THE
RED
CAMP

EMILY

The memories come to me on cool, dry October evenings when the Santa Anas whistle and dance through brittle pepper tree leaves and the glowing sunset radiates a final burst of brilliant orange-blue. Curling smoke from a backyard fire surrounds me, and in the distance I see the small, tar-tiled houses of El Campo Colorado clustered against the dark rolling hills of La Vista. Weary, sweat-stained men and women trudge slowly up the dusty streets while barelegged, brown-skinned children play a game of tag in the vanishing light. Rhythms of a twice transplanted Spanish blend with the strains of an impassioned ranchera *song and together, rising above the wind, dance upwards into the atmosphere, leaving behind the echoes of a people—laughing, fighting, loving and crying.*

LAS HIJAS
THE DAUGHTERS

Emily:
Not My Sister

The Red Camp is where I live with Mom, Dad and my three sisters: Gloria, Rita "La Chiva" and the baby Laura. I'm the third one, the third girl. Mom says she wants a boy next, but I think Dad wanted a boy before.

Mom calls me the quiet one. Gloria, who's the oldest, is the friendly one, and Rita, who's two years older than me, is the troublemaker. That's why she's nick-named "La Chiva"—she's stubborn and mean just like a goat. We don't know what Laura is yet because right now all she does is cry. I tell Mom I don't like being the quiet one, but she says that's what I am and so that's that.

We've lived in the camp for as long as I can remember. When I was real little, Dad worked in the groves and we lived in the small wooden camp houses. Now we live in the barrio, and Dad has a job at the tire factory where Mom says he makes good money

Sharon, my best friend in Mrs. Paulsen's class, is not allowed to come to the camp because her parents tell her it's not a good place. I'm not sure what that means, but ever since then when I talk to Americans, especially the kids at school, I don't tell them I live in the camp, because it's not like in the heights where they have big houses or even like Sharon's house where they have sidewalks. Instead, I tell them I live on Buena Vista Avenue, which is a very long street, and most of the time they don't ask me anything else.

Mostly Mexicans like us live in the camp. My teacher taught me to say Mex-i-can, not Metz-i-can, like I used to say. She said, "You're from Mexico, not Metzico."

Except we're not from Mexico, we're from here. But we're not Americans because Americans are white. We're Mexicans from America. It's confusing. And because I look different, people are always asking me what I am. Sometimes I say Spanish, because Spaniards speak Spanish and my Mom and Dad and older sister Gloria talk in Spanish. But then, La Chiva says I can't be Spanish because I'm too dark. "Spaniards are from Europe and they are white like me," she says. I hate her when she's like that. Rita is pretty and really light, and Mom says Rita knows this, and that's why she acts like the devil.

Mom tells me I take after my Dad—*prieta como una india*. Dark like an Indian. Because of this, Gloria and Rita tease me and do stupid things, like give me the black cereal bowl and tell me I'm not their sister. At first, I believed them and cried so hard that I fell asleep, exhausted, outside in the mustard field next to our house. When Mom came home from work and found out what happened, she spanked Rita and Gloria really hard and then went out looking for me. She found me still asleep in the field, all wet and shaking from the mist. Rita really got in trouble for that one, but then she's always getting in trouble for something.

What Gloria and Rita don't know is that I'm REALLY not their sister. Like in the tiny-print, yellow-paged fairy tale books from the bookmobile, a band of gypsies kidnapped me from my castle in Spain. They taught me how to fly and took me all over the world. Then all of a sudden they left me here. I don't know why they flew away, but I do know my real parents have sent people out looking for me. It's just a matter of time.

Each night, while Gloria and Rita are asleep on each side of me in our swimming pool bed with the big dip in the middle, I lift myself up, float out through the open window and into the camp. I soar through the neighborhood, searching for the gypsies who know the way back home. And this is how I know certain things. Like, which men come stumbling out of El Veracruzano late at night and which boys hang out at Los Arbolitos, playing horseshoes in the dark and putting pennies on the tracks to give to their girlfriends the next day. It's how I know what time Tía Legunda starts cooking *menudo* on

Saturday nights and when Cuni, Jessie and Rufiano drag in to eat it.

When I fly over Blackie and Helen's small blue house, I see them throw each other against the thin walls, rattling the windows like a sonic boom. And when I pass over Tía Neche's, I see her sitting on her wooden porch, smoking cigarettes one after another while she waits for Tío Manuel to come home. Sometimes I see Dad driving the station wagon home, slowly weaving down the street, coming from a place Mom calls "who knows where."

When the night is almost over, I sweep down low over my friend Martha's house to wake up her rooster and then slip quietly back through the bedroom window and land safely in the dip without even waking up my two sleeping stepsisters.

That's how I know I'm not their sister. Because I can fly and because soon I will find those gypsies and be on my way back home. And besides, I don't even look like them. I look like a Princess from faraway Spain.

Gloria:
La Botella y el Corazon
The Bottle and the Heart

I watch Carmen from a far corner near the living room window. She sits all scrunched up on the sticky brown naugahyde couch and puffs really hard on her cigarette, then looks at the clock—again. *Yo sabia que no iba a venir.* I knew he wasn't coming. At five o'clock, when Carmen said to get ready for Petunia's birthday party, I told her we didn't have to hurry, that he wouldn't be here...at least not on time. *Pero ella es sorda.* She just doesn't listen. So I went ahead and put on my new blue-striped jumper with the black skinny belt and my new black patent-leather shoes. And now I have to take them off.

"Why do we have to wait for him? Can't we go with Tía Mercy or Tía Clara?" Rita whines.

"Rita, be quiet! And Gloria, help your sisters put their pajamas on, right now."

"I *told* you he wasn't coming home," I say.

Estoy tan enojada. I'm mad at Dad for not showing up and mad at Carmen for being so stupid to believe he'd be on time, when he's never been on time. I get mad at Carmen a lot. I think that's why I started calling her Carmen instead of mom. When I call her Carmen, it's almost like she's someone else and then I don't get crying mad, just regular mad. But Carmen doesn't like it when I call her Carmen. I think that's another reason why I do it.

Carmen's eyes get real little and she looks away. Reaching into her purse, she pulls out another cigarette. I feel bad because she looks like she wants to cry, and it's my fault. But she should know by now.

I help Rita and Emily get ready for bed, and then I go back into the living room. I tell Carmen I'm not sleepy, so she lets me stay up and sit with her. We watch TV and I comb her long wavy hair. For every gray one I pluck, she gives me a nickel.

It is late now. Midnight. Carmen's cigarettes are all gone. I don't want to leave her alone, so I play cards on the living room floor and Carmen pretends to read her *True Stories*, but I can see she's only staring at the pictures.

I feel myself being picked up. "No."

"What do you mean, no?" she asks. "It's late, it's time to go to bed."

"I want to stay with you. Please, I was just resting my eyes."

She laughs and lays me on the squeaky couch. She places my head on her lap and her long fingers smooth my hair.

▻◇◅

A loud banging wakes me. Carmen jumps up and runs to the kitchen door.

"¡Carmen, *abre la puerta*! It's Manuel, *tengo a* Emilio!

It's my Tío Manny and he sounds scared. I hear other voices, and as I walk into the hallway to hear better, I see, stacked near the front door, Carmen's battered cardboard suitcases and three grocery bags full of my and my sister's clothes. I hear the kitchen door open and Carmen screams. I run into the kitchen and see my Tío Jessie and Tío Manny holding my Dad. He is bleeding all over them and the black-and-white checkered floor. A large piece of broken glass sticks out of his neck. They sit him down on a kitchen chair, and Carmen puts a dishtowel with dancing spoons against his neck. It turns dark red.

"Why didn't you take him to the hospital?" she demands as she reaches for the phone.

"He didn't want to go," says Jessie. "He wanted to come home. There was some trouble at the bar."

"¡*Pendejos!*" she curses at my *tíos*. She dials quickly, connects to an ambulance service and gives garbled directions. She hangs up. Tears stream down her face as she places another towel against my Dad's neck. No one sees me staring from the corner.

"No llores," my Dad mumbles. Carmen cries harder. I start crying, too. The blood soaks through the towel and is now dripping on the floor. My Dad's head rests on his chest. I think he is going to die.

"¿Qué pasó en la cantina? And tell me the truth, okay!" she shouts at my *tíos.*

Jessie looks at the floor. "He got in a fight with a wetback."

"About what?" she asks.

Jessie glances at Tío Manny. "I don't know, something stupid."

Carmen looks at them. She knows they're lying.

"I swear I'm going to kill that barmaid," she utters bitterly.

I hear the siren in the distance, and soon it's in our driveway. My Dad's head falls to the side.

"Carmen, *mi amor*..."

"Sí, Emilio, I'm here."

"I'm dying. *No me dejes,* don't leave. If you leave me, I will die. *Te quiero mucho."*

Carmen sighs heavily. "I'm not leaving," she says quietly.

The ambulance attendants enter through the front door, pushing aside the pile of suitcases and bags. They quickly place my Dad on the stretcher, and Carmen and Tío Manny follow them out.

As the ambulance pulls out of the driveway, my Tío Jessie lights a cigarette and inhales deeply. He notices me for the first time.

"He's going to be okay. *Ve a dormir*."

"I'm not sleepy."

He sees the pile of suitcases and bags. "Are those your Mom's?"

"Yeah."

He exhales slowly.

Placing a blue suitcase under one arm and grabbing a bag with the other, he motions toward the others.

"Why don't you help me put them away."

Rita La Chiva: *Maldita* Bad Girl

No way I'm going home.

When the final bell rings, instead of lining up for the bus with the other kids, I sneak out the back way through the playground. The one time Mom found out I walked home from school, I got in real big trouble, so now I make sure she never finds out. I like walking home. There's lots of things to see, and it's more fun than being on the bus with those stupid scaredy babies who don't like walking because it takes too long and they get too tired. I don't mind it at all.

Once I leave the school, I hopscotch down Olinda Street, turn right on Rose and go downtown on Central Avenue to the Sprouse-Reitz Five and Ten Cent Store, where they have all sorts of neat things. Pretty plastic see-through purses, high-heeled sparkle shoes like Barbie's, ribbons and barrettes and all kinds of lipsticks. I steal a tiny tube of red lipstick and a shiny gold jack set and slip them into my pocket. No one even notices.

Next door at O'Brien's Jewelry, I jump up and check the window display that changes each month.

In December, tiny elves polish piles of sparkly diamonds in a dark cave, and in July a glittering American flag made of rubies, sapphires and diamonds twirls round and round a silver pole. My favorite month is March, when the leprechauns dance around golden pots filled with dark-green emeralds. Today a shiny silver ferris wheel spins little buckets of pearls through the air. Whatever O'Brien's has, you can be sure it's going to be something you want to take home and keep for yourself. I just haven't figured out how to do that yet.

At Central Drugs, I weigh myself on the scale and then smell all the perfumes on top of the glass case. Jungle Gardenia and Miss Dior are my favorites. The crabby lady at the cash register stares at me, so I leave and go to Carl's Liquors, where I buy a purple Charm pop from a nosy man who asks me if my Mom knows where I am. I say yes, yes, she does. He says it's getting dark and I should go home. I lie and say I am—after I visit the grocery store and read the comic books, and after I say hello to the dogs on Orchard Street, then maybe it will be dark enough so that the stupid baby-sitter will be gone and Dad will be home from work and already snoring on the couch, and then finally Mom will come home from the packing house. Then maybe I will go home.

Emily:
In the Camp

Gloria and Rita hate the camp and want to move. I don't. Martha Estrada, my best friend, lives in the camp, too, and understands why, why I like the smell of the wet dirt after it rains and the sound of the mean freight trains as they speed by at night, shaking the tiny camp houses like an earthquake.

Martha has a short pug nose, straight black hair and a pushed-in chest that makes her breathe kind of funny. Other kids tease her, but I don't say anything because Martha never says anything about my hand-me-down clothes or my English mixed with Spanish.

Martha lives four houses away from me on Buena Vista in a low white brick house that stays cool all summer. Chickens, ducks and a cow live in her back yard, and a giant pepper tree that we like to climb grows in the front.

Martha loves the camp like I love the camp, and we have a game that goes like this:

Me: In the camp we don't have sidewalks.
Martha: But we have fields of wild mustard, where we play hide-and-seek.

Me: In the camp we don't have swimming
      pools.
Martha: But we have Coyote Creek, where
      you can catch tadpoles and minnows.
Me: In the camp we don't have streetlights.
Martha: But we have bonfires that light up
      the sky.
Me: And in the camp we have *raspadas*,
      cool and sweet like cherries that make
      your mouth so happy, you lie down on
      your mama's lap and then nothing mat-
      ters—not the Tiny Tears you couldn't
      have for Christmas, and not the trip to
      Disneyland Dad never showed up for,
      only Mom's fingers slowly scratching
      your back and making you sleepy.

And the game goes on and on for as long as we
want or until Mom calls you in for dinner.

Rita La Chiva:
La Llorona
The Crying Woman

I was playing statue with Gloria, Emily and my cousins Darlene and Karen in the back yard of my Tía Eva's house when I first heard about La Llorona. Because I had made fun of her stupid ballerina pose, Darlene swung me extra hard across the yard, and I fell, careening down the hill and towards the creek.

"Hey, come back, don't go down there," yells Darlene as I roll to the bottom of the hill. "La Llorona might get you!"

Landing at the edge of the creek bank, I lay still, pretending to be hurt.

"Rita, come on, get up!" she shouts.

I don't move a muscle.

"PLEASE, get up!" she screams as she starts down the hill towards me.

I finally laugh and roll over.

"*Mensa*," she curses from above, "I hope she gets you."

I race back up the hill after her. "Who's supposed to get me?" I ask breathlessly.

"La Llorona. She's a witch who steals mean girls like you, Chiva. Haven't you guys ever heard of her?"

Gloria, Emily and I look at each other blankly. We shake our heads no.

"Come on, tell us about her! Or maybe you're just making it all up?" I tease.

"Forget you," Darlene angrily says as she turns to walk away.

"Please!" I beg. "Come on, Darlene. I'm sorry I faked you out. You can walk home from school with me next week."

Darlene, who is spoiled and kind of bossy, doesn't have many friends, and I know this will get to her.

Her face lights up. "Okay, but it has to be two weeks."

I nod my head reluctantly.

"Come on, this way," she commands.

We follow her out of the back yard, past a pile of abandoned tires, through a tall row of hedges and into a field choked with waist-high weeds. She leads us to an abandoned camper sitting in a far corner.

"In here," she whispers. "It's getting dark and we don't want to be outside if she comes."

I roll my eyes at Gloria, who smiles back at me. Darlene can be so stupid sometimes.

We huddle underneath a musty olive-green sleeping bag as Darlene deadbolts the camper door. She takes one final peek out the window and begins:

"Okay, umm...a long, loooong time ago, before La Vista was here, way before Santa Ana and Anaheim and even Olvera Street were here, there lived a Mexican family, named Alcalá, who owned a huge *rancho*.

"Fernando, the Alcalá's only son, fell in love with a young Indian servant girl named Luisa, who was very beautiful but also very dark-skinned. Fernando's parents didn't approve of Luisa, so the two were forced to see each other secretly. Well, it wasn't long before Luisa wanted to get married. Fernando knew his parents would never give their blessings, so he kept giving Luisa excuses, you know, like he needs more money or his mother is sick, or it's a bad time for him, whatever. And Luisa, because she was so stupid from love, believed him. Even Luisa's own mother told her to stay away from Fernando, that he would only break her heart. But Luisa didn't listen. She was in love.

"Years pass and Luisa and Fernando settle down and have three children. Fernando builds a *casita* for his new family, but he doesn't live with them, instead he stays with his parents in the big ranch house. This doesn't make Luisa happy, but she's still hopeful some day they will marry and, anyway, what can she do?

"One day Luisa passes the tiny church and sees a huge wedding going on. You know, everyone's happy and eating *mole* and listening to the musicians, and so on. She moves closer to get a look at the happy couple and sees it is her Fernando marrying his cousin Cecilia Alejandra Luz Marina de La Peña, a dainty, light-skinned, wealthy *señorita*. Well, Luisa is mad! Her mind goes crazy and she thinks about chopping him up into little tiny pieces and throwing him into a pot of stew, but then she remembers she still loves him. She runs home, crying every step of the way. In her little house she sits and thinks and thinks and thinks and finally decides what to do—she will get even."

"That evening, late at night, Luisa takes her three sons down to the creek. She kisses them tenderly then leads them into the cold, dark water. As the creek deepens, the children cry, but Luisa doesn't stop. She walks in until their tiny heads are underwater. The struggling boys quickly tire and sink to the bottom of the creek.

"The next day, the small bodies are found floating in the creek, and the news spreads fast through the *rancho*. Everyone searches frantically for Luisa, but she is nowhere to be found. When Fernando hears about the children, he is so upset he takes his hunting rifle from its glass case and shoots himself in the head.

"And then a really weird thing happens. Shortly after the drownings, people report seeing a strange sight near the creek: a beautiful, dark-haired woman dressed in white floats above the creek bank, moaning and crying. When they try to approach her, she vanishes. And then children begin mysteriously disappearing. The people say the crying woman, La Llorona, is Luisa gone mad, and it is she who takes the children, believing they are her own. And even today, when kids are bad and stay out late, La Llorona grabs them and takes them down with her into the deep, black water."

It's dark outside and we are all quiet inside the camper, our ears straining to hear crying sounds in the wind.

Darlene turns to me. "And if you don't believe me, go ahead, go down to the creek. I just hope you can swim."

"That's a really stupid story," I angrily say.

"Any smart person would have killed him, not the kids. That's what I would have done. And I don't believe Luisa drowned her kids. She wasn't mad at *them*. They didn't do anything wrong." I stand up and push open the camper door. "And there's not even enough water in Coyote Creek to drown anybody. I'm going down there right now and check!"

Jumping into the darkness, I hold my breath, run down to the edge of the creek to prove them all wrong and then race back to Tía Eva's kitchen, never daring to look back.

Later that night as Dad drives us home in the bright moonlight, I'm still thinking about La Llorona. If what she did was true, she must have been real mad. I wonder if Mom will ever get that mad.

That night I dream of baby fish. Not baby FISH but little, HUMAN babies, the size of goldfish with little fins and tails and tiny, crying open mouths.

Gloria:
Staying

I hear Carmen and Tía Mercy arguing in the kitchen. *Como perros.* They've been fighting a lot lately and it's making me crazy.

Tía Mercy says she's tired of hearing Carmen talk about it. "You say you're going to do it, but you never do," Tía snaps.

"I know, I know. But it's the money. You know I don't make enough at the packing house," Carmen answers.

"Well then, stop talking about it."

"He just makes me so mad! He doesn't come home for days, and then everyone in the camp knows more about what he does than I do. I won't put up with it. I'm going to kill him first and then I'm going to burn down the cantina!"

"Carmen, you know it's not the cantina and it's not the money. It's not even the women," Tía Mercy says.

"Then what is it? Why can't I just leave?" Carmen sighs heavily.

I peek into the kitchen and I see Tía Mercy looking deep down into her coffee cup before she

lifts it slowly to her lips. Why won't she say anything? Why won't she tell Carmen the truth?

"It's you," I whisper to Carmen under my
breath as I tightly grip the door frame. "It's all your
fault. You're the reason you can't leave."

Emily:
Second Grade

I feel sick. I asked Mom if she would call school and switch classes for me, but she said no. Now I'm stuck in Mrs. Perry's second-grade class for a whole year.

"She's the meanest teacher at Emerson," Rita yells as I watch her hopscotch down the driveway. "Elvia says she hits you on the hands with her pointer and then makes you stand in the corner. And she's the hardest teacher, too."

My stomach hurts.

Mom calls us in for dinner. She sets a plate down in front of me.

"Just beans and cheese," I remind her.

"I know, I know," she says as she places a *tostada* on the plate.

"Mom?"

"*Sí.*"

"Rubén is in Mrs. Clark's class and, if I'm in that class, then I can help him."

"*Ay*, Emily. You'll learn a lot from Mrs. Perry. She can't be that bad."

"She is," says Gloria. "She's so mean none of the other kids will walk by her classroom because she yells at them. They say she locks her students in the paper closet when they can't answer a question."

"Gloria, that's enough, *la vas a asustar*! I don't want to hear any more about it!"

I am already scared. Mom doesn't know Mrs. Perry, and that's why she doesn't believe Gloria. Mrs. Perry is tiny and walks with her head sticking out, like a little dog being pulled on a leash. Her hair is twisted back in a tight little bun, and she wears black heavy shoes like the sisters at the church. But the scariest thing about Mrs. Perry is her stare. When she looks at you, you feel like you've done something really bad, even if you haven't.

I don't tell Mom this, but the main reason I'm afraid of Mrs. Perry and her class is because I don't know her rules.

Once you learn the secret rules of school, it's okay. They're secret because no one tells them to you; you just kind of learn them by making mistakes. If you stick to the secret rules, bad things won't happen. One of the rules here at Emerson School is not speaking Spanish. Gloria's teacher hit her on the hands with a ruler when she spoke Spanish. Now Gloria hardly speaks it at all. Another rule is don't bring *burritos* in your lunch. Just don't be different. I think I am getting good at not being different. But I slip once in a while. Like in Mrs. Turnquist's class, when I couldn't think of the English word for "cousin," and so I sat there not saying anything at all because I knew if I said *primo*, Mrs. Turnquist wouldn't know what I meant and would tell me to speak English. It just makes you feel dumb.

⊨◇⊣

Stupid, stupid. That's what Dean, who sits in the desk in front of me, calls me. Dean is really smart in math, and I am not, so each day he reminds me HOW stupid I am. To me math is a different language, not like the words in books that I can't wait to read. Sometimes math is so hard it makes me cry. But I don't, because I know Dean is right there in front of me, waiting for me to cry.

Dean makes fun of a lot of people. Especially people like Donna. But then, most people make fun of Donna. Donna looks like one of the angels in my catechism book, with long golden hair, blue eyes and soft white skin, but she smells like something else. Her nickname is Donna Peepants, because she always wets her pants. Mrs. Perry makes Donna sit in the corner of the classroom because no one can stand the smell.

⊨◇⊣

During recess, Martha and I are doing turn-
overs on the bar, and Donna stops and watches.
Martha wrinkles her nose and moves away towards
the monkey bars. Donna looks at me and I point to
the bar. "Go ahead, your turn."

She jumps on the bar, hooks one leg over,
straightens her back and whips herself up and over.
Once, twice, four times forward and four times
backward. She returns to the top and pauses, takes
a deep breath, then flips forward and backward
without hands.

"Wow," I say, "that's good."

"Thanks." Donna smiles, her small teeth re-
minding me of tiny, yellow corn kernels. She jumps
off and pats her dress down over her stained underwear. The bell rings, and Donna slowly walks away
towards our class line-up, looking not at the other
kids but down at the ground. I follow her towards
the line. Behind me I hear a familiar voice.

"Pew, pew Peepants!" It's Dean.

Donna ignores him, but I see her shrinking into
the ground.

"Dopey Donna pees in her pants. Where's her
bottle!"

"Shut up!" I yell as I turn around and face
Dean.

Dean and his gang laugh.

"Stupid and Dopey are friends now. Are you
guys going to get married?"

I kick dirt in Dean's direction, and he laughs harder. Donna looks at me with a sad look in her eye. She doesn't want me to make a big deal.

"Jerk," I say to Dean.

"Dumbbell," he answers.

"Idiot."

"Fart-face," he spits back.

"Retarded jackass."

He pauses, not sure how to answer this. His face reddens. Mrs. Perry rounds the hallway and approaches the line.

"Line up quickly," she commands.

"You, you...stupid fucking Mexican!" he shouts.

Mrs. Perry stops abruptly.

"Dean!" she barks.

"*¡Pinche cabrón!*" I shout.

Mrs. Perry looks at me. Oh, no. I'm going to get in trouble. Tears fill my eyes. But instead, Mrs. Perry turns, grabs Dean's arm and drags him away towards the main office. I am so relieved, I sob. Huge, gasping sobs. Donna gives me a funny look and then lines up beside me, smiling.

Rita La Chiva:
Menudo

I don't like *menudo*, but I like watching my Dad and Tío Chema eat it. Tía Flora is my Dad's favorite sister and he likes to visit her on Sundays when he is hungover. So almost every Sunday we all pile into the station wagon and drive out past the grasshopper oil derricks to Placentia.

Because Tía Flora knows Dad is going to be *crudo*, she makes sure she has a huge pot of *menudo* ready. Mom won't eat it, because in secret she tells us she can't eat any *menudo* she hasn't seen prepared. Something about how some people don't know how to clean tripe.

I like the smell of *menudo* and the taste of the nutty hominy. But I don't like the meat. It slips and slides in your mouth and gets caught in your throat and makes you want to throw up. So instead of eating, I sit in the corner of the kitchen and watch. Tía Flora serves Dad and Chema big bowls of steaming *menudo*. They add a squeeze of fresh lemon juice, some diced white onions and a sprinkling of oregano. Then they slowly roll a fresh flour tortilla, dip it into the soup and take a bite. They chew once, twice, and swallow. Then they add a heaping spoon-ful of menudo to their mouths, lean back in their chairs and enjoy. That is how you eat *menudo*.

Emily:
Bless Me Father

I go to CCD every Saturday morning during the school year because Mom makes me. I'd rather stay in bed and watch cartoons, but this year I make my First Communion, so I can't miss any classes.

I'm excited about my First Communion because I get to pick out my white dress and shoes and because I also finally get a rosary and a missal. I have to memorize a lot of prayers to get them, but I don't mind, they're easy: OhmygodiamhardlysorryforhavingoffendedtheeandIdetestallmysinsforthyjustpunishmentbutmostofallbecausetheyoffendtheemylordwhoartallforgivingIfirmlyresolvewiththehelpofthygracetosinnomoreandtoavoidthenearoccasionsofsin.

Last week, Sister Margaret told us we would have confession rehearsal today. She said we must think of all the sins we have committed and tell them to the father in the confessional booth. As we all line up outside the booth, I'm thinking real hard... What have I done?...something bad... Nothing. I haven't done anything bad, or at least I can't remember it. As I get closer to the front of the line, I get nervous. My cousin Rubén bursts out of the confessional smiling.

"Now my mom can't tell me I'm going to hell!" he whispers to me.

"What did you say?" I ask, hoping to get an idea.

"I'm not telling you. You'll tell my mom!"

I'm almost at the front of the line. I'm shaking.

I raise my hand. Sister Margaret walks over.

"Yes, Emily," she says.

"I can't think of any sins," I shamefully whisper.

She looks at me hard and then sighs deeply.

"I will help you remember. Let's see, have you talked back to your parents? Or lied, or cheated on a test? Stealing something is also a sin."

She pauses and looks down at me. I stare at her blankly. She tries again. "You could also say taking a cookie without permission is a sin."

That's it. My sin. I nod my head solemnly, and she nods hers, both of us in agreement. I am indeed a sinner. I enter the booth, ready to confess and be forgiven.

"Bless me father for I have sinned, this is my first confession and these are my sins..."

Laura:
Baby Chicks

Last night Gloria told me that Mom's in the hospital. She said Mom's brain is bleeding. Rita says there is something in her brain that shouldn't be there and they have to take it out. What are they taking out? A piece of the brain? No, not her brain, just something.

Dad's real quiet. He doesn't play with me anymore like he used to. He just sits in the big chair and watches TV. I ask Gloria if he is mad at me, and she says no, he's just worried. Gloria is kind of like the mom now, except she doesn't cook. Tía Mercy comes over and makes us food. I'm glad because Dad only knows how to make Campbell's Tomato Soup.

Gloria says I can't go see Mom in the hospital because I'm not old enough. But Tía Mercy says I can go on Easter. Easter seems far away.

I sit on my bed in the dark and think about Easter without Mom and I start crying. Gloria comes in and tells me to go ahead and cry more. She says I need to get it all out. I cry but it still stays inside.

⊳◇⊲

On Easter we all get dressed up and go to Sambo's Restaurant and have pancake breakfasts. Four girls and my Dad. After eating, we go to Saint Joseph's Hospital and see Mom. She wears a little yellow bed jacket and has tubes in her arms. She has bruises all over and she is skinny and looks tired.

"Did they take it out?" I ask.

"No, they dissolved the tumor," she answers.

"How?"

"They put needles under my arms and pulled it out."

I picture the doctors pulling a tumor from underneath her arms and it makes no sense. I whisper to Rita that I don't understand what Mom means, and she tells me not to worry about it, Mom's confused.

After the hospital, Dad drives us home and we play with our baby Easter chicks. We each get one, except for Gloria, who doesn't want one. We take the box of chicks out on the porch and let them run free. I watch mine all the time, making sure he doesn't fall off the steps. Rita's chick starts pecking at mine and my chick pecks back. Back and forth and back and forth they go, each time the pecking getting meaner. They're hurting themselves, I tell Rita. No they're not, they're playing. But I don't believe her. The chicks' peeps get louder and louder as tiny down fluffs fall off their bodies. I think they're killing each other. I tell Rita and she says I'm crazy. Get them away from each other, I beg her. She doesn't listen. I'm too afraid to separate them, thinking they'll bite me with their sharp beaks. I try nudging them apart with my shoe, but they keep pecking at each other. Rita, make them stop! She doesn't and instead walks away, bored with the chicks and me. I can't watch them anymore. I have to make them stop! I step on my baby chick and squash him. Shaking, I slowly lift my foot. He doesn't move. I run to the laundry room, back into the corner and hide. Why did they have to fight? Why did they have to hurt each other? I wouldn't have stepped on him if he didn't fight.

Rita La Chiva:
Liz Taylor

"Mom, Tía Clara looks like Liz Taylor."

"What did you say?"

Mom is reading *Photoplay* and on the cover is a heavy, shiny-faced Elizabeth Taylor, holding a glass of wine.

"See," I say as I point to the magazine cover. "Tía Clara wears big Hawaiian muumuus, and drinks a lot, like Liz Taylor."

"You're crazy."

"Yeah, she does. And Liz Taylor has a round face, big, black caterpillar eyebrows and puffy hair, just like Tía Clara."

Dad laughs his giggling hiccup laugh and Mom acts mad.

"Ay, Rita," she says.

"But she really looks like Elizabeth Taylor when she eats pomegranates. Her face gets all shiny and sweat drops from her forehead. And she breathes real hard, like Lucha's pig. Do you think Elizabeth Taylor breathes hard like that?"

"*Maldita*," Mom says. "I'm going to tell your Tía what you're saying," she says in between laughs.

Dad winks at me.
What did I say?

Emily:
The Farm

I didn't notice Dad was gone because he is hardly ever home. He works so much, and lately he's been staying away from home sometimes one, sometimes two nights, that I didn't even notice he'd been gone for a week. And no one said a word.

><>=

One morning as I am leaving for school I see Dad's clothing—his pants, shirts, socks, underwear—all folded neatly and stacked on our Spanish-style red velour sofa.

"Mom?"

She comes out of the kitchen and sees me staring at the clothes.

"I'm taking those clothes to your Dad today. He's in jail."

"What happened?"

"He got in another crash," Gloria answers from the dining room as she fills her mouth with cereal.

"I'm going to see him this weekend. Do you want to come?" Mom asks.

"Uhm, maybe...I have to go now. I'm going to miss the bus."

I rush out the door feeling embarrassed and mad. Why is Dad always doing things like this? I hope Gloria and Rita don't tell any of my friends about this.

⊨◇⊣

With Dad gone, everyone relaxes, even Mom. We don't have to be quiet all the time, we can watch whichever TV show we want, and I can invite my friends over and not worry about him showing up. I feel kind of bad about liking that he's not here. Mom says he'll be gone for nine months. That's a really long time.

⊨◇⊣

On Sunday morning Tío Vicente and Tía Clara pick us up and drive us out to a place they call the county farm. Gloria is excited because Dad wrote her a letter asking her to sneak in a small jar of Tres Flores hair pomade for him. She has the jar with her and is going to toss it into the irrigation ditch once we get inside. We drive past the entrance, and it does look like a farm. Tío Vicente slows down. Gloria leans out and throws the jar into the ditch.

"I hope this doesn't get us into trouble," Tía Clara grumbles. Tía Clara doesn't like Dad.

"Clara, it's just pomade," Mom says. "What can he do with that little jar?"

"Cut someone's throat," she answers.

Mom sighs and stares out at the rows and rows of small green plants.

Passing the fields, we drive down a long, dusty road lined with eucalyptus trees. Mom told me about Dad's accident earlier, and I can't stop thinking or dreaming about it. She said it happened late at night and Dad had been drinking. He was driving down Western Boulevard and, as he crossed Laurel Street, he drifted across the center divider and crashed head-on into a Volkswagen Bug. Both cars flipped and Dad's truck rolled over into a side ditch, right next to the Drive-In. His side door flew off and he landed safely in the street. The truck exploded seconds later. The other driver died instantly. To keep my mind off the horror, I play a different version of the accident over and over again in my head. In my version, Dad escapes from the flames and saves the other man's life. Then, from a distance they both watch as the vehicles explode, sending metal, glass and shattered beer bottles spraying across the street.

The men file into the large meeting room filled with relatives seated at long tables and benches. I try to think of something to say to him. He wears a baggy blue cotton jumpsuit and looks thin. I am afraid of Dad. Afraid he might not like me, that I might not say or do the right thing to please him. Mom tells me I am like Dad. That bothers me.

Dad sits across from us. He doesn't seem sad to be here. He smiles and hands out presents. For Mom, he has a leather wallet tooled with beautiful roses on one side and "Carmen" on the other. My sisters get belts and I get a small leather coin purse.

Tía Clara is quiet during most of the visit. Tío Vicente jokes with my Dad and tries to keep everyone happy, but then Mom starts crying. Gloria, Rita and I say nothing.

A bell rings and it is time to leave. I am happy to get out of there. Sometimes I wish I had Martha's or even Sharon's dad.

I later find out that Dad never got his Tres Flores. A few days before our visit, Gloria had written him telling him where she was going to throw the jar, but what she didn't know was that the guards read all the letters. Maybe they found the jar or maybe somebody else picked it up. Either way, Dad never got it.

Gloria:
Fortune Cookies

"But you told me on the phone that you had a car!" insists an irate Mr. Han.

"No, I didn't say that," I answer red-faced. "What I said was that my dad lets me use his car practically anytime."

"No, no, no! I heard you say you had your own car. That's why I asked you to come in for a interview," he replies impatiently.

Taking a deep breath I feel myself break out in a sweat as I awkwardly attempt a second lie to cover up the first.

"Look, I'm really sorry if I confused you, but I promise, getting to work on time is never going to be a problem. And in a few months my dad is probably going to give me his car when he buys a new one."

Mr. Han glares at me and then sighs.

"Okay, okay. You're hired. The hours are Tuesday through Sunday from 3 p.m. to 10 p.m. You'll be working the cash register.

"I'll be here right after school," I answer.

"That means no football games or other school stuff, you know that, right?"

"Yes."

"And this is okay with your parents?"

"Yeah, no problem, they don't mind," I reply, lying again.

"All right, you start tomorrow. Buy your uniform tonight at Nenos Department Store and memorize the names and prices on this menu. You get $.95 an hour, a half-hour break for dinner, and meals are free. And no switching hours with the other girls. Any questions?"

"No."

"Okay, see you tomorrow at three."

I smile stupidly and stumble my way out of the small Chinese restaurant. *Híjole*, man, money! I run down Hillhurst Avenue, thinking of all the different ways I can spend it: First, I'll have to give some to Carmen because the money from the farm is not enough, then a coat for Laura who only had a sweater all last winter, and then some new school shoes for me.

By the time I reach Buena Vista I have a whole new wardrobe and a sports car. Then all of a sudden—damn! I have to buy the uniform tonight and I have only six dollars from baby-sitting! If I borrow some money from Tía Mercy for the uniform, then use my baby-sitting money for the work shoes—that'll work. Now the car problem. Even if Dad hadn't wrecked the car I couldn't have driven it because I'm not old enough to have my license. I guess I can ride Emily's bike to school and then to work. I'll have to park it away from the restaurant, so Mr. Han can't see it. Yeah, that's what I'll do. Now, all I have to do is convince Carmen to let me work. That'll be the easy part.

Emily:
Racing

I draw horses. Over and over and over again until each arch of the neck, curve of the flank and angle in the fetlock is perfect. Horses are all I think about. I draw them, study them, collect all sizes of horse figures, from plastic cowboy and Indian horses to delicate bone China statues from the TG&Y.

Mrs. DeAngelis, my sixth-grade teacher, has asked Janine, Stacey and me to stay after school. She wants to know why every day before school, during recess, after lunch and sometimes even after school, she sees the three of us running around the fields like we're crazy. I don't want to say anything, but she threatens us with detention. So Stacey steps up and tells her about the secret club we formed and how we're practicing real hard to make the next Olympics. Mrs. DeAngelis smiles and says she's very proud of us. Janine and I say nothing, marveling at how easily Stacey can lie.

Our club is not really about the Olympics. We
don't talk about it much, but I think it means something different to each one of us. Our club is kind of
like a family. A family of horses. And we race
because we love to run. We've even made up our
own club symbol, which is a large triangle with
three small triangles, each small one intersecting
one of the three angles of the large triangle. In the
center of the large triangle is the letter "A" for Ara-
bians, our club name, and in the center of the small
triangles is the initial of each of our secret names.
Mine starts with "S" and that is all I can say.

We told our good friend Patty Maloney about
the club, and she didn't really understand. Patty
likes horses, but she doesn't love horses like we do.
When we told her we ARE the horses, she looked at
us really weird. I knew we had to stop then. So I
laughed and made a joke and said, "Not really," and
Stacey and Janine laughed, too.

"How could we possibly be horses?" Stacey
roared.

Patty laughed along with us, a kind of crooked,
unsure laugh.

But we are the horses. Or rather, we become
them.

We each have a stable of 25 horses, each horse
with it's own name, personality and racing style.

Stacey has the long-distance runners. She trains them by running the length of the entire playing field over and over again. She can run forever. Stacey has a deep chest, strong lungs and comes from behind like most good distance runners. But lately her ankles have been bothering her, and we've been discussing getting them fired.

The sprinters belong to Janine, who holds the 50-yard dash record and who has calf muscles like small hams. My horses are the middle distancers and I have long, lean legs, strong quick feet and good timing.

Over and over again we race our horses up and down the field, building our strength, increasing our speed and practicing in the winter rain and during the long smoggy summer months.

I guess we are kind of nuts about this, but we do it because we have to. When I'm running, the earth is a part of me. The wind urges me on and the grass springs up below me, lifting me upward and onward. Sometimes I run so fast, I feel I'm galloping on all fours, flying low, devouring the ground. When I'm running nothing else matters. The sun, the mist, the smells take over. I disappear.

Gloria:
María del Veracruzano

It is the middle of the night and Carmen wakes me up. "*Levántate*, I need you to drive me to the cantina."

I am furious because ever since I bought my 1964 Mustang with the money I earned working as a cashier at the Mandarin Kitchen, I've become the family chauffeur.

"Jesus Christ, why do we have to go now?" I ask.

"Just get dressed, we have to go. Hurry up!"

I dress, and soon we are driving the few blocks to the cantina. I don't ask what this is about, because I already know. Ever since Dad got out of the County Farm and started working nights at El Veracruzano, Carmen's been acting really weird. She gets all worked up and then asks me to take her out looking for Dad. I want to say no, but for some reason I just can't.

As we approach the bar, we hear music blaring out the front door. Men drift outside to smoke and hang out. I park directly in front of the bar, and Carmen jumps out of the car.

"Stay here and lock the doors," she says. She enters the bar and I lose sight of her in the crowd.

I look around me. The streets are empty. The men near the entrance stare at me. I want to throw their looks back at them, but instead I avoid their gaze.

Suddenly I hear a scream, followed by cursing in both English and Spanish. Men stream out of the double doors. I see Chueco, the bartender, dragging a struggling Carmen out the door. She jerks away from his hold and runs back in. Another scream. I jump out of the car and into the crowded entrance.

"*¡Puta, pinche cabrona!* I'm going to kill you!" I hear Carmen shout. I squirm into the doorway and what I see amazes me.

Carmen and the barmaid are on the ground. Carmen holds the woman's red bubble wig in one hand and with the other holds her down by the throat. She tosses the wig onto the bar and then grabs the woman's hair. The barmaid squirms away, but Carmen chases her through the bar and into the bathroom. The barmaid locks the door and Carmen pounds on it.

"*¡Sal de ahí, puta!* Come out now!" she yells.

Dad grabs Carmen and pulls her outside, kicking and screaming. I see him walk her around the back of the building, trying to calm her down.

My Tío Jessie walks out of the bar and towards me.

"What are you doing here?"

"I drove Carmen here."

"Come on, get back in the car. I'll follow you back home," he says. Carmen continues to curse in the background.

"Okay," I answer, somewhat relieved.

I drive back to the house, and Tío Jessie follows me to make sure I get in all right. About an hour and a half later, I hear a car door slam and Carmen enters the house. I hear the car drive away. I try to fall asleep.

The next morning, Carmen cooks breakfast like nothing has happened. I look out the window—one sure way to know if Dad came home or not. The car is there. But barely. Sitting on its rims, all four tires are shredded. I wonder if it's Dad's recklessness or Carmen's anger. Either way, I guess it doesn't matter. She found him and they made it home.

Emily:
Model Houses

Dad is in construction now and he knows where all the best model houses are. Sometimes on Sundays we'll all pile into the car and drive out past the groves all the way to Yorba Linda or Irvine to look at the houses. Because he works on them, Dad has keys to some of the models and we get to go inside. They are beautiful. Smelling of fresh paint and newly cut carpet, they sparkle like diamonds. La Chiva and I have a routine: before we walk inside, while we're standing out on the porch, we close our eyes and hold our breath—it's always better that way. And when we open our eyes, the lights inside are all soft and glowing, like in your dreams. La Chiva usually then races up the stairs to the bedrooms so she can choose hers first. I wander into the kitchen and imagine smelling *arroz con pollo* or hearing the clap-clapping of Mom's hands when she makes tortillas. As I walk through the living room, I see myself coming home from school, putting my books on the coffee table and curling up on the sofa to watch TV.

The nicer models have shimmering chandeliers and silk flowers in elegant vases. Sometimes we'll find one that has quiet music playing in every room, like it's coming from the walls themselves.

After Chiva and I choose our bedrooms, we inspect and assign every room in the house and then move to the outside. The back yard is usually just an empty lot filled with dirt, so we pass that by. The garage and driveway are always bright white without oil stains or broken-down cars, and I imagine seeing Dad there, helping Mom on weekends around the house.

In the front yard Rita does cartwheels and makes huge dents in the new, soft, green grass. I sit on the curb and look across the street at the empty houses that stare blankly back at me—lonely and cold—waiting for someone to move in. Waiting for a family like ours.

Driving home from the models, I am sad. It would be nice to live in a new house. From the back seat of the station wagon I watch the sun jump back and forth like a jack-in-the-box through the tall rows of eucalyptus trees. As we get closer to the camp, I see my friends playing out in front of their small houses. And I feel a little guilty—these houses aren't that bad. They just look a little tired, kind of like they're ready to sit down and relax after a hard day at work.

Rita La Chiva:
Party Time

When I grow up, I'm never acting like they act. Like Mom and Dad. Like the way they were last night.

It started when Tía Mercy and Tío Gilbert and Tía Clara and Tío Vicente came over on Sunday to visit. They sent Emily, Hector, Rubén and me to the movies. By the time we got back from seeing *It's a Mad, Mad, Mad World*, Vicente Fernández's voice was roaring out of the stereo and Tío Gilbert had already gone out to get more beer.

Emily lowered the stereo volume and went into our room and locked the door, like she always does. I turned on the TV and found *Pillow Talk*, one of my favorite movies. Gloria was still at work, and Hector and Ruben, knowing better than to stay, had already walked home. So I stretched out on the couch and enjoyed the movie.

A few minutes later Mom walked into the living room.

"Who turned down the stereo?" she asked.

"I don't know. Emily, I think," I answered, not taking my eyes off of Doris Day.

"Damn her."

Mom turned up the stereo volume and walked back into the kitchen.

"Rita, are you hungry?" she asked from the kitchen.

"No, I had a hot dog at the movies."

"Did Emily eat?"

"I don't know," I answered, irritated.

Mom came back into the living room and sat down beside me. She smelled like beer and cigarettes.

"Rita, go to the dairy and get me a pack of cigarettes."

"Mom, no, I don't want to, ask Dad. I'm watching a movie, and besides, they won't let me buy cigarettes."

"Okay, be like that," she said. She kissed me and then clumsily walked out of the room.

I guess I fell asleep after that, because the next thing I remember is Gloria waking me up and telling me to go to bed. The voices of my parents and aunts and uncles were loud. Gloria still had her white nylon uniform on and smelled like Chinese food. The sound of shattering glass exploded through the air, and Gloria and I looked at each other. She ran out to see what happened. My back stiffened. Damn them. I pulled the red velvet couch pillows over my ears and sank down into the couch. I didn't want to hear any of it. But Mom's sobbing, screeching voice cut through the cushions.

"*¡Desgraciado, hijo de puta!* You don't care about me, you don't care about anyone but yourself."

I heard Dad laugh, uncomfortably.

"*Cálmate*, Carmen, it's okay. You'll wake up the girls," Tío Vicente said soothingly.

"Just leave her alone, she's not going to try anything," Dad half-joked.

"*Cállate*, Emilio," Tía Mercy warned. "She's really mad."

I heard another beer bottle breaking, followed by scuffling. I walked into the hallway and saw Mom run into the kitchen and pull open the silverware drawer. She grabbed the largest and sharpest knife.

"You say I'm not going to kill myself. Well, just watch me. You treat me like shit. You don't want me around. Well, you don't have to worry about me, *cabrón*, *mentiroso!*"

Mom raised the knife above her wrist just as Gloria grabbed her arms from behind. The blade cut into Gloria's hand.

Gloria screamed.

Dad grabbed Mom's hand and the knife dropped. Gloria fell to the ground crying, and Tía Mercy started screaming at my Dad.

"My sister, my sister, you're killing my sister!"

Tía Mercy punched Dad. Tío Vicente came in to pull her away. Tía Clara watched all of this from the doorway, shaking her head.

Dad took Mom, still screaming, into their bedroom. Gloria walked, hunched over, to the sink. I helped her rinse the blood off. A surprised Tío Gilbert stepped into the kitchen with two six-packs and took in the mess.

"Carmen's crazy," he whispered.

"No, she just had too much to drink," said Vicente. "We've all had too much to drink."

Dad came out of the bedroom.

"Gloria, are you okay?"

"Yeah, but it's still bleeding a little."

Dad looked at the cut. "I don't think you need stitches."

I looked at Dad and then at Gloria. "Why do you guys always do this!" I shouted. They all stared at me like I was the crazy one. "This stuff always happens," I shrieked. "You're all idiots!"

I ran out of the kitchen and into the bedroom, locking the door. I put my Aretha Franklin album on as loud as I could. I listened for a few seconds, breathing deeply, trying to catch my breath. It didn't work. I slid the window open, pushed out the screen and pulled myself up and out. I had to get out.

Emily:
Other People's Parents

I spend a lot of time at Stacey's and Janine's houses.

Stacey lives on Edna Street, a block away from our school. Her small green house is dark and cool and filled with books and magazines. Stacey's parents, Mr. and Mrs. O'Donald, went to college and like to drink martinis. Sometimes they even take Janine, Stacey and me with them to fancy cocktail lounges and order us Shirley Temples. Mrs. O'Donald is really smart and goes to graduate school. She calls herself a feminist. Mr. O'Donald works in a big office in downtown Los Angeles and likes to cook, but he doesn't get much of a chance because he's always working.

Because Stacey's parents aren't home most of the time, she gets to cook her own meals. Her favorite meal for breakfast, lunch and dinner is steak and Coca-Cola.

Janine's dad, Mr. Richardson, works at the Chrysler Plant and comes home every day at 5 p.m. Mrs. Richardson stays at home and cooks real American food, like mashed potatoes, spinach and macaroni and cheese. I like Mr. and Mrs. Richardson a lot because they're really nice, but sometimes they look at me like they're worried, and it makes me uncomfortable. That's why even though I like being at the Richardsons' house, I prefer to go to Stacey's, where no one watches you or asks you anything.

A lot of times I wish my parents were more like other people's parents. But they're not. So when being at home makes me feel sad or mad or lonely, I just walk over to my friends' houses. Mom doesn't like it much, though. She says I spend too much time away from home.

Emily:
I Think I Love You

Laura lives for TV. She's ten-years-old and she can tell you what's on any channel any time of the day.

She watches everything. Starting in the morning with "Gumby" and "Rocky and his Friends," and then continuing after school with "Hobo Kelly," "Speed Racer" and "Kimba the White Lion." On weekends she watches the really stupid stuff, like the "Banana Splits," "HR Pufnstuf," and "George of the Jungle (watch out for that tree!)."

Laura even has her snacking scheduled around the TV. Every weekday afternoon at the 4 p.m. commercial break, Laura goes into the kitchen, pulls out five slices of Oscar Mayer bologna and carries them into the living room, where she knows she's not supposed to be eating. She lies each piece of bologna on top of the couch arm. One, two, three up one arm. One, two up the other. It's really gross. Then one by one, she slowly devours the pieces, first stripping the outer rind with her front teeth, spiraling it into her mouth, then nibbling away at the remaining circle by turning the shrinking center of meat round and round and round. She finishes the last slice by 5 p.m.

But Laura's favorite programs come on at night. She loves "Bewitched," "I Dream of Jeannie" and "Here Comes the Bride," but her all-time favorite is "The Partridge Family." Laurie, Keith, Danny, Tracey and that obnoxious little boy. Those little eggs and birds at the beginning and that "Come on Get Happy" song make me sick, but she loves them. When she watches "The Partridge Family," she gets this real happy look on her face, like it's her birthday or something. I think Laura believes she is a member of the Partridge Family. Mom bought her the Partridge Family album for Christmas, and when she can't watch TV, she stands in front of our bedroom mirror and plays it over and over again, lip-syncing and pretending that she's playing the keyboards, just like Laurie. She plays that album so much, I can hear the songs in my sleep.

I like to watch TV, too, but sometimes I wonder about Laura. There are times when gazing at the screen she appears to slip into a trance. She gets real still and quiet. Not quiet like me when I'm being mean or when I'm afraid and don't know what to say, but quiet like she's real far away, with that shine in her eyes and her voice softly humming, "I Think I Love You."

Emily:
Give and Take

"Egg salad, again!" I moan as I remove the mushy, warm sandwich from its plastic baggy. Egg salad sandwich, potato chips, an apple and a Ding Dong. The same lunch every day. Janine checks out my lunch as she thoughtfully chews her bologna, Frito and mayonnaise sandwich.

"Where's Stacey?" I ask.

"In the cafeteria," Janine answers with mouth half-full. "I'll take the Ding Dong if you don't want it."

Janine, Stacey and I are nerds. I think that's why we've remained best friends for so long. Stacey, who is tall, skinny and flatchested, wears a mouthful of braces, and is tough and hardheaded. Sweet, naive Janine is petite and curvy, has long, dishwater-blonde hair that never seems to be washed often enough, and wears glittery blue cat's-eye glasses that sit halfway down her nose. I'm tall and skinny like Stacey and so backwardly shy that I don't think

I've spoken up once in class this year. I think it is our sympathy for each other that keeps us together.

"I hate those guys," Stacey whispers from behind us as she slips her thin legs through the metal table bench and plunks her lunch tray down on the table. We follow her gaze to a nearby table where Cheryl Mann, Marla Madigan, and the rest of the pep-squad bunch gather for lunch.

"Well, you're not alone," I answer.

"But they're really nice...most of the time," Janine says in their defense.

"Yeah, most of the time," I sarcastically answer.

Stacey digs into her spaghetti and I watch her gaze wander back to the nearby table.

"Stacey. Stacey!" I shout.

"What!" she snaps as she turns sharply toward me.

"Why are you paying attention to them? You don't even like them!"

"I'm just watching! Just leave me alone, okay?"

I look at Janine, who shrugs her shoulders. I pull out the second half of my sandwich.

"Hi."

Looking up from my lunch sack, I see a tall varsity-jacketed Jeff Hauser towering above me.

"Hello," I answer.

"So I hear you're in the Honor Club?" he asks.

"Yeah, so what?" I answer nervously.

"What else are you in?"

"Why do you want to know?" I ask.

"I just want to know if you'd like to run for student body president, because I'd like to be your campaign manager."

"Me?"

"Yeah."

"Why?"

"Well, I know I don't know you that well, but I like you and I hear you're really smart and are involved in a lot of things like the yearbook and sports. Stuff like that. And I think you'd make a good president."

I glance at Stacey, who looks skeptical. Janine sits wide-eyed and open-mouthed.

"Hmmm,..." I answer. "I think I have to think about it."

"Okay. Well, let me know tomorrow, okay?"

"Okay."

Jeff joins his basketball friends, and together they walk away in a pack towards the cafeteria. I reach into my sack, pull out the Ding Dong, carefully unwrap the foil cover and sink my teeth into the spongy chocolate cake.

"What are you going to do?" asks Stacey.

"What do you think I should do?" I say faintly.

"I think you should do it. He wants to help you," Janine chirps.

"Yeah, but why does he want to help me?"

"There's something disgusting about him," Stacey comments.

"I think he's cute," says Janine.

"On the other hand, there's a lot of things you could do as president," adds Stacey.

"Like what?"

"Shorten the cafeteria line. Let girls wear pants to school..."

Janine cuts in, "Get better equipment for the girls hockey team, abolish P.E. showers...."

I jump in, "Longer lunch periods, shorter classes and make cheerleading illegal!"

Janine, Stacey and I explode in laughter.

"Well, at least I could try, right?"

"Right," they answer.

"Mom."

"Yes."

"What do you think of me running for president of Lincoln Junior High School."

"*M'ija*, I think you should do anything you want to do."

"No, Mom," I say exasperatingly. "I'm asking if you think it will be a good idea for me to do it."

"If that's what you want to do."

That's not what I want to hear, but that's the way Mom is. It's always "Whatever makes you happy *m'ija*." I want her to tell me, yes, do it, it will be good for you, or, NO, don't do it, it's a big mistake. I want someone to tell me what to do. I get tired of making all the decisions.

When I ask my sisters for advice, Gloria says do it, Rita warns me to stop bothering her, and Laura says I should run for cheerleader instead. I don't ask Dad.

I decide to run. I say yes to Jeff, and immediately he's making plans.

"We have one week to campaign, then next Monday we give our speeches and later that day we vote. On Tuesday, you'll be president. We need to start now. We need posters, banners, handbills, rallies..."

I beg Mom for money to buy art supplies. Together Stacey, Janine and I create ten posters, three ten-foot butcher-paper banners and one hundred mimeographed handbills. During breaks and lunch periods, Jeff stands on a table in the lunch plaza and gives speeches praising my qualifications and promising I'll make a great president. He's cute and funny and everybody loves him. He's so good he sells me on myself. Still, every now and then I wonder why he's doing this.

Monday arrives and I am terrified. The students fill the amphitheater. Jeff gives a funny introductory speech and then it's my turn. I stand and nervously read my short speech from carefully written index cards. And then it is over. The students go wild and give both of us a standing ovation. I return to my seat and collapse against Janine and Stacey. They tell me I did good. Somehow, something doesn't feel right.

⊨◇⊣

The following morning, during homeroom, the winners are announced. I am named president.

⊨◇⊣

At break I track down Ellen Hauser, Jeff's younger sister and a friend of mine from elementary school. I find her out near the back of the school, sneaking a cigarette with her girlfriends.

"Hi, can I talk to you for a second?" I ask her.

"Sure, hey, congratulations on winning."

"Thanks," I say quickly. Ellen has always been nice to me. With her pudgy body and too-loud laugh, she is kind of an outcast herself.

We walk away from the group and I blurt out, "Ellen, why did Jeff help me win?"

"What do you mean? He was your campaign manager; he wanted you to win," she answers.

"No! Why did he ask me to run, why did he want me to win?"

"That's a stupid question. Didn't you want to win?"

"Yeah, but...I mean, he didn't even know me. And I'm not really a part of that crowd, you know."

I look at her and I remember the chubby first grader who was out half the school year with pneumonia. She never really seemed to catch up after that.

"Please, Ellen," I plead, "you know what I mean."

She looks down at her unlaced sneaker and gives in.

"Well, I don't know why, but Jeff really hates this school and he wanted to mess with it and leave it in bad shape. Electing a Mexican girl president was one way of doing it. But you know, I don't know, it seems like he kind of got to like you, and after that he campaigned because he wanted to. Jeff likes to win. I don't know, he's my brother, but he can be kind of a jerk sometimes."

I run out into the baseball field, feeling ashamed and angry and stupid. I hate him. I stop in the middle of center field and sit down and cry. How can I face them? I'm a joke. My mind races. Maybe I can quit. Or maybe I'll transfer out. I lie on the cool grass and close my eyes wishing I could disappear and never see any of these people again. Instead I see the whole amphitheatre in front of me, filled with laughing and jeering faces. In the distance, I hear the the first bell ring and I will my body to leave, float up into the air and fly far away. Feeling lighter and lighter, I open my eyes and see below me

the playing fields and the tops of the school build-
ings. Then the tardy bell rings, loud and shrill, and
I'm down on the field again. Wiping my eyes with
the back of my hand, I shake the grass off my dress
and reluctantly head back towards class. As I walk
down the hallway, students warmly congratulate me
and suddenly it hits me—it doesn't really matter.
Jeff will graduate in two weeks and be gone forever.
People voted for me and I won. I guess we both got
what we wanted. I was not only going to be president, I was going to be a good one.

Rita La Chiva:
Light My Fire

I really, really, really hate it here. Especially now, in August. It's boring enough during the rest of the year, but in August this town becomes hell. It's so hot, even the tiles give up and slide right off the roofs.

No way I'm waiting. Before Mom left she told Emily, Laura and me to wait here for Dad and he'd take us to the Corn Festival. "He went to Tío Manny's and he'll be back in an hour," she said. Yeah, and like I still believe in Santa Claus. If he's not here by three o'clock, I'm leaving. I'll walk to the Corn Festival by myself. It's only a couple of miles. I'm almost fourteen, anyway. I shouldn't have to be going anywhere with my parents or my stupid little sisters.

It's three o'clock and I tell Gloria that I'm going over to my friend Theresa's house. Gloria warns me that if I go to Theresa's, I won't be able to go with the others to the festival. I can't believe she really believes they're going. She's so stupid. Sometimes she acts just like Mom, or maybe it's that she wants to get rid of us so she can spend time with her boyfriend. Emily and Laura look up from their game of Fish as I walk through the living room and out the front door.

"We'll bring you back a present from the Festival," Laura says, hoping I'll change my mind about going with them.

"No, that's okay," I answer guiltily, knowing that I will definitely go and their chances are slim at best. I run out the door, jump off the porch steps and into the street.

I run a block and then walk a block. The sweat drips off my face and neck, running down my chest and drenching my T-shirt. Damn. I'm going to look horrible when I get there. I have on my new sleeveless, cropped, white-ribbed T-shirt with my blue bell-bottom jeans from Jeans West, because even though I'm meeting Theresa at the festival, I'm really going to see Jess. Jess Vargas is a junior whom I've had a crush on all year. He goes to La Vista High School and lives two blocks away from us, near the railroad tracks. I'll just have to sneak into a bathroom somewhere and clean up. Run, then walk. Walk, run. I pass El Rey Bakery, Foster's Freeze, Ray's Auto with the monkey mechanics on the billboard, and finally the library, which sits right before the park.

Theresa sits on the curb corner eating a buttered corn on the cob.

"Why do these idiots call it the Corn Festival? They don't grow corn here. It should be the orange or lemon or even the avocado festival."

"I don't know," I answer. "How long have you been waiting?"

"Forever. I thought your Dad was driving you here."

"No, I walked."

Theresa tosses her cob into the gutter, stands up and straightens her short denim skirt around her muscular brown thighs, then readjusts her halter top over her bulging cleavage.

"Come on, I saw Jess and his friends over past the game lines. He's been waiting for you."

At the mention of Jess's name, I reach for the Saint Christopher medal hanging from a chain around my neck. Jess gave it to me last week while we were eating *taquitos* at the Foster Freeze. When he asked me to go steady, I wasn't sure what to say, so I told him I needed to think about it first before giving him an answer. But I took the medal anyway, because I like the heavy chain and the feel of the cool silver disc on my skin.

Jess and I haven't really done anything. We haven't held hands, kissed or even really talked that much. I guess this is kind of like our first date.

I follow Theresa through the game area, where guys try landing shiny dimes onto smooth flat plates or struggle to toss white featherweight plastic balls into tiny fishbowls, all in the hopes of winning a lime-green teddy bear or a tiny, scared goldfish. We push our way through the cotton candy, corn dog and burger lines, and finally reach the picnic area.

"Rita!"

I turn towards the voice and see Jess peering out from a group of bushes. We walk through an opening in the bushes and find ourselves in a small, private clearing surrounded by trees. Jess and his two friends, Rudy and Anthony, stand in the center of the clearing, drinking from a small bottle. Jess hands it to me.

"Tequila," he says. "Have some, it's great."

I look at Theresa, but she's already busy drinking from a beer can, so I take the amber bottle from Jess and drink. A slow, strong warmth slides down my throat. I pause, catch my breath and take another drink. In the distance, a battle of the bands plays "Light My Fire." I like this.

Jess and I wander through the crowds, holding hands. We get on the ferris wheel and soar over the park. The sun is setting and the festival neon lights flicker on. Our basket stops at the top of the wheel and Jess and I sit there gently swinging back and forth in the warm breeze. I don't ever want to come down.

⊏━◆━⊐

"Rita... Rita!"

From the ground I look up into the air, following Theresa's voice.

"There," Jess points, "she's on the Octopus."

Theresa leans out of an Octopus arm and points.

"What's she pointing at?" Jess asks.

"I don't know."

I follow the line of her arm. "Maybe she wants us to meet her at the half-apples. That's where she's pointing."

We slowly make our way through the crowd to the half-apple line. I stop abruptly.

"What?" Jess asks.

A few yards away I see Dad, with a paper bag in his hand, helping a vomiting Emily and a screaming Laura off the half-apple. Laura clutches a half-eaten corn dog while Emily holds what looks like a bag of peanuts to her chest. Gloria comes out from behind the safety fence to help Dad. I can't believe he fed them before getting on the rides! I pull my hand out of Jess's and run away into the crowd. Jess calls out after me, but I keep running. I hide behind the House of Horror.

"What's wrong with you, why'd you run away?" Jess asks minutes later as he catches up with me.

"My Dad. I don't want him to see me."

"Why not?"

"Because I'm not supposed to be here alone," I answer rudely.

"Are you going to get in trouble?"

"I don't know," I snap. I'm mad at them all: at Jess for asking stupid questions; at Gloria for giving in to Dad and coming here; and at Dad for carrying that paper bag.

"I don't know if I'm getting in trouble, and I really don't give a shit."

Jess stares at me, confused for a second, then shakes his head and slowly smiles. "You're something else."

Behind us "Light My Fire" wins another applause battle, and the organ intro starts up again. Jess pulls out the tequila bottle and I grab it from him, gulp quickly, then take his hand and lead him away from the festival and into the street.

EL PADRE
THE FATHER

Emilio:
Waiting

It's ten p.m. when I pull my truck into the parking lot of the Hungry Lion Coffee Shop, drive to the far corner behind two palm trees, turn off the ignition and wait. Through the trees I watch the waitresses closing down the restaurant as they move from table to table refilling salt and pepper shakers, cleaning booths and wiping down tables. Gloria is one of them. She laughs and jokes with the other waitresses. She looks happy. Today is her seventeenth birthday and I haven't seen her in over a year. I admit it's all my fault. I could have seen her and her sisters, and I actually have set out to see them. Only, when I get there I start feeling really uncomfortable, like I don't have enough...of anything. And so I leave before even getting to the door.

A year ago, I moved out of the house because I couldn't live there anymore. I still don't really know why I left. Carmen doesn't know why either. It was for a bunch of half-reasons. We'd been fighting for so many years, I think she just expected it to go on like that forever. But I couldn't do it. I can't change what I am, and she was always wanting me to. Sometimes I think that even if I wanted to change, I wouldn't know how. I felt bad then and I still feel bad, so I guess leaving didn't really help all that much. I hear Carmen didn't take it all that good.

I send Carmen money whenever I can, whenever I'm working, but I'm not always working. Construction has slowed down, and you have to keep going further and further out to find the sites. And then there's always someone younger and hungrier willing to work for less. Work has been so slow that I went to Mexico for a while and then came back and moved in with Jessie and his new wife Lois, out in Palmdale. I like it out there in the desert. You can think, you can breathe. Orange County used to be like that, but now it's all cement and people. The fields, orchards and groves are gone.

I see Gloria sitting down at a table with the other waitresses. They're counting their money. I hope she did good tonight. Carmen tells me Gloria wants to go to college, and that's why she's saving her money. I wish I could help her. I wish a lot of things were different. Sometimes I wish I didn't drink so much.

It's like Jessie says, sometimes *la vida no vale nada*. Life isn't worth shit. But I really can't complain. Sure, I've had bad luck, but I've had more than my share of good times. It's just sometimes those really hard times take the will out of you. Like when you have a job that breaks your balls, but you can't quit because your family needs to eat or, even worse, when months go by and you can't find a job for the life of you. Or when you realize that it only gets harder as you get older. If there is a God, He sure didn't make it easy for us.

I see Gloria putting on her sweater and getting ready to leave. She walks outside and heads towards her Mustang. I start the truck and drive towards her.

"Gloria."

She turns towards me, recognizes me and smiles. *Gracias a dios.*

"Hi, what are you doing here?"

"Happy Birthday."

"Thanks."

"So, where are you going now?"

"I'm going out to eat with my friends."

"Oh, okay. So...how's your mom?"

"She's okay."

"That's good."

It's cold outside, and Gloria clutches her sweater tightly.

"Well, I'll let you go."

"Dad," she says softly.

"Yeah?"

She twists the top button of her sweater and her mouth tightens up real small. She looks like she's going to cry. I knew I shouldn't have come.

"Dad, thanks for coming. I just want to tell you that I love you, okay?"

I'm surprised. Caught off guard. My chest hurts.

After all I've done, and she tells me that she loves me. *Carajo*.

"Well, I better go now, they're waiting... bye." She turns and walks towards her car.

"Have a fun time with your friends," I manage to say as I shift into gear and slowly pull away. As I exit the parking lot, I see her in my rearview mirror, standing alone in the empty lot, watching me leave. *Te quiero, también, m'ija*. I love you, too.

LA MADRE
THE MOTHER

Carmen:
Destiny

I watch Emilio Reyes Cruz, in his freshly starched and pressed army uniform, move down the street like an alley cat with his head lowered, eyes staring straight ahead and his long legs gliding real smooth underneath him. Heading towards his father's house in El Campo Colorado, he crosses 4th Street and glances up at me on the steps of my Tía Julia's porch. I pull my skirt up just a little bit, slowly moved my legs from underneath me and stretch them out full-length in the warm sun. He smiles.

I always dream the beginning the way it really happened. The way we met. It's the ending I dream differently, sometimes better, most times worse. The dreams with happier endings, where Emilio and I stay together, leave me feeling depressed and angry—for being such a *pendeja* and for still having hope when everyone knows your destiny is your destiny and you can't escape it.

I'm tired. For months now, I've been keeping watch. Making sure they don't get too close. But they're smart. They followed us when we moved from the house to the apartment and sometimes they've even knocked on the front door, pretending they're the apartment manager or the Avon Lady or even schoolkids selling candy. But I'm good at watching. I stay up day and night, keeping them away. Watching and thinking.

"Ay, m'ija, *stay away from that one. He's got girl-friends all over the place." Tía Julia stops sorting the beans and looks me straight in the eye. "I see you watching him. Better not let Clara find out. She can't stand the sight of him."*

"¿Y por qué no?"

"He's wild, he's trouble and he's a Cruz. Clara thinks the whole family is stuck-up. And on top of all that, I just heard he got kicked out of the Army. If I were you m'ijita, *I'd forget about him."*

I think a lot about the past. People and places that are gone. Like the flower fields I worked in when I was a girl or my father's shotgun house in Colton. I think about death, too. Mostly my own. The doctor Rita takes me to wants me to see another doctor about the voices. But I tell him, hell no, I'm not crazy, I don't need that kind of help.

"Are you ready?" Clara yells from the hallway.

I look at myself in the mirror. I'm looking good. Low-cut red V-neck sweater, tight black ankle-slit skirt, suede platform shoes and ruby-red lipstick. ¡Ay que chula! *Emilio and I made a plan last week to meet tonight at the Harmony Ballroom Halloween Festival. I thought today would never come.*

"Almost."

Clara enters the small bedroom and her eyeliner-perfect eyes widen.

"¡Carmen, pareces una puta! *You look like a whore! Can you even breathe in that?" she asks.*

"I'm not changing," I announce, glaring back at her.

"Sin vergüenza," *she utters as she shakes her head. "You have no shame. At least wipe off some of that lipstick. And hurry up, Vicente is waiting in the car."*

The ballroom is beautiful: Red and gold streamers unfurl from the ceiling like silky corkscrew curls while people in their Saturday-night best slowly fill the hall. A large band performs on a spacious stage, and in the far corner a bar serves soft drinks and beer. I scan the faces and most everyone is from La Vista or Fullerton. I see La Coqueta Linda Velásquez in her padded push-up bra flirting with the newly married Ernesto Gómez. La Gordita Ginny Luna and her two skinny sisters anxiously eye the men across the room, hoping they'll be asked to dance. Out on the dance floor Chueco and my cousin Esther shout insults at each other as a small group of men egg them on. Most of the guys, including Emilio's four brothers, stand together near the exit, drinking beer, listening to the music and watching the crowd.

I spot Emilio in a dark corner, surrounded by a group of girls. Leaning back against the wall, I place my hand on my hip, strike what I think is a sexy pose and wait for him to notice me. He doesn't. I shift my hips. Still no response. Frustrated, I finally walk over to him.

Emilio beams as I approach him. Bending to kiss my cheek, he whispers in my ear, "¡Ay, mi vida! ¿Por qué te quiero tanto?"

I smile sweetly and narrow my eyes. Glancing quickly at each other, the other girls quietly move away. We're alone. His lips brush my face and he whispers in my ear again. I know I can't believe a word he says. But it is nice to hear.

Across the room I catch Clara watching us. Strains of "Moonlight Serenade" fill the ballroom as she makes her way towards us. I grab Emilio's arm and pull him onto the dance floor. Emilio grins as he watches Clara disappear into the crowd.

"So I heard you quit the Army?" I ask.

Emilio's eyes crinkle as he chuckles, "And who told you that?"

"My Tía Julia."

"Well, Tía Julia's wrong. You can't quit the Army; I went AWOL."

"Why?"

"I didn't like it," he answers seriously.

"And what didn't you like?"

"We were treated like slaves. Worse than in the fields. And besides..." He smiles. "I missed you."

"¡Ni me conoces! Maybe it was someone else you were thinking of," I sharply answer.

He playfully kisses my neck, and I think if the Army is worse than the fields, then I don't blame him for leaving. Emilio's worked the fields since he was six-years old. He hates them more than I do.

The song ends and Emilio gently presses his body against mine. ¡Que mal hombre! Tía Julia was right, what a ladies' man.

"Let's leave," he whispers.

Emilio pulls me out the door, through the crowd outside and into the parking lot. We stop at a dark blue Chevy, and he pushes me up against the door and kisses me. Soft, slow and deep.

"Oye, cabrón," I whisper as I push him away. "I have to get back. Clara saw us."

"Come on, let's go for a ride."

"I can't."

"Ay, mi amor, vamos no más por una hamburguesita."

"I'm not hungry."

"Mentirosa. I don't believe you," he softly utters. He looks at me, smiles, and his hands, deep golden brown and heavily calloused, slowly button my *sweater. I close my eyes and he softly kisses each eyelid.*

"All right," I sigh quickly, "let's go."

We get in, he starts the engine, and the Chevy races out of the parking lot.

The frayed living room curtains flutter and I snap awake. The smell of blood fills the apartment. Heavy breathing. There are so many of them. They exhaust me. I reach for the knife under the sofa cushions and listen. They're whispering about me. I shout at them to stop and, grabbing the knife, I run to the front door, throw it open, and scream *"¡Cabrones, no me van a agarrar!"* Neighbors peek out their windows, too afraid to open their doors. I slam the door shut and pray to God to help me.

We speed through Anaheim and Fullerton towards the camp. The night sky is blue-black.

"I thought we were getting something to eat."

"Pues, I guess I changed my mind. Nothing seems to be open, anyway," Emilio answers.

Looking across at him, I wonder if he's telling the truth.

"So then where are we going?" I ask.

I tell Rita to drive me to East Los Angeles, to the flat part right before the hills. My cousin Lupe gave me the address of a woman who will help me, *una curandera*. When Rita and I walk into the small living room filled with waiting patients, they move aside and make way for me to walk through. *La Curandera* peeks her tiny, shriveled face through the doorway of the bedroom, looks at me and waves me into the room. She hands me a towel and tells me to take off my clothes and lay down on a small bed. I do as she says. Her strong hands rub my body with an ointment that smells like mint and rose petals and I feel my muscles relax. I want to cry. I ask her what is wrong with me but she doesn't answer. Instead she prays and takes an egg, a tomato, and a lemon and rolls each over my body.

"*Alguien la quiere ver viejita*," she finally says to me. "Someone wants you to be an old woman."

"*¿Quién?* I ask.

"*Alguien.*"

Who? Who would want to hurt me? And then I think of the Mexican woman Emilio is seeing.

Emilio turns left onto Buena Vista, crosses the railroad tracks and enters El Campo. The tiny barrio is asleep. We drive up a pot-holed dirt road to one of the small wooden houses.

"*I'll be right back*," *he whispers, jumping out of the car.*

He runs up the dirt path, leaps onto the wooden porch and reaches for the door. The door opens suddenly from the inside and Emilio faces his father, Don Antero, who stares first at Emilio and then out at me in the car.

I hear arguing in Spanish. Don Antero sounds furious. Emilio abruptly turns and walks back to the car.

"What happened?" I ask as he opens the door.

"He won't let us stay here."

"You asked him if we could stay here? I can't believe you! Take me home, now!"

Emilio slides into the driver's seat and turns to me.

"Carmen, let's go to Yuma. To get married."

"Married? ¿Estás loco or what? Is this a joke?" I ask.

No reply. He stares at me, waiting for my response.

I turn away and look out the window. What is he saying? Does he know what he's doing?

I look back at Emilio. I see the high Indian cheekbones, the green, taunting cat's eyes. Who is this man I think I'm in love with but whom I know little about, other than he likes to drink and he likes women? I get embarrassed and look away. Closing my eyes, I try to think it all out, but instead I feel the springs in my Tía's lumpy sofa, the hot sun of the flower fields, the slap of my father's hand. And the need and desire in Emilio's eyes.

"Okay... vamos," I say. He starts the engine, and we head towards Yuma.

When she is finished, *La Curandera* hands me the lemon, egg and tomato in a crumpled paper bag and tells me to throw it away as far as I can. I don't know if this means as far as I can throw or far away from where I live, so I decide to throw it in the trash bin of the market we stop in before we leave East Los Angeles. I heave the bag with all my strength and then get back into the car, where Rita stares at me with a face filled with fear and worry. She thinks I'm out of my mind.

"*Vamos*," I say, "let's go home."

She starts the engine and we head back.

EMILY

Emily:
Volver, Volver
Return, Return

It's not easy for me to come back. I'm returning home for my younger sister Laura's wedding and, although I'm only an hour away by plane, I've made a point of keeping my distance. Several years ago, before I left for college, Dad had moved out of the house and disappeared into Mexico, and Mom was hearing voices and talking to herself. Since both Gloria and Rita had married and moved out, I was next in line to take over. I quickly bailed. College provided an escape from family responsibilities, and I was thankful. Unfortunately for Rita and Laura, my departure meant they had to carry the weight of my father's final abandonment and my mother's bitter and self-destructive anger.

Even though I'm back for just a few days, I'm still looking to escape, still hiding out. All I want to do now is stay out of the storm and then head back up north.

"Do you think he'll come?" Laura anxiously asks Gloria and me as we sit in Gloria's kitchen, eating our lunch of tuna fish sandwiches and chicken noodle soup.

"You know Dad," Gloria answers, "I wouldn't count on it."

Not too long ago, Gloria heard from the relative grapevine that Dad had returned from Mexico and was living with his brother. Laura called Dad at Tío Jessie's and asked him to be in her wedding. He accepted. And now, one day before the wedding, she's nervous about it. And with good reason.

"I told you you should have done what I did," Gloria says gently.

When Gloria got married, she avoided the whole "Dad" situation by asking an older male friend to give her away. Everything went smoothly and Dad, even though he was a little late, did show up for the wedding. He didn't seem to mind being replaced, but then you never really know with him.

Laura chews on her lower lip and looks at me. "What do you think?"

"Maybe you should have a backup just in case."

I am not in the wedding, and that's okay with me. At first I was hurt because Rita and Gloria were asked and I wasn't, but then I realized I couldn't afford it anyway. I'm in graduate school, an Art History major, and I'm completely broke. Art History. It never sounds quite right. Whenever I tell people my major, a voice in my head tells me to get real, who am I kidding, someone like me can't afford the luxury of Art History. I should have gone to law school or med school, you know, Help The People. The great brown hope that wasn't.

The wedding is being held at the new Our Lady of Guadalupe Church, which was built next to the old one. The new church is all sunshine, air and light-colored stained glass. Folksy, guitar strumming melodies replace ominous Latin chants. Gone is the mystery, the sadness. I miss the darkness.

I wait inside the church entrance and watch the relatives file in. It's hard to tell our family from the groom's. Mike, Laura's husband-to-be, comes from a longtime camp family, also. We could almost be the same family, but I can hear Mom disagree. "They're shorter and darker." She dislikes Lola, the groom's mother. Stems back to an old fight over a boyfriend. Mom says Lola was a big flirt and still is.

My Dad's four brothers and three sisters—Tíos Jessie, Manny, Oscar and Mario and Tías Flora, Eva and Gaby—are all here with their grown children. My mother's aunt, Tía Tomasa, the matriarch of the Ruiz family, arrives with her daughters and all my cousins from Victorville. No one lives in the camp anymore. They have spread out all over Southern

California: Fullerton, Santa Ana, Westminster, Placentia, Anaheim and Brea.

The organist begins to play. I walk down the aisle to the front pew, genuflect, cross myself and slide onto the hard bench. I look back. Still no sign of Dad. What did I expect? Laura must be out of her mind now. Everyone is seated and the wedding party nervously waits at the entrance. Mike's brother escorts Mom down the aisle, and Lola follows with an usher. Mom turns into our pew and sits beside me. I watch her as she kneels.

"He's not here yet, huh?" I whisper.

"Well, what did Laura expect?" she answers.

The music swells and the four bridesmaids and ushers walk down the aisle, followed by my nephew Philip, the ring bearer, and my niece Andrea, the flower girl. Mike enters and smiles nervously as he approaches Father Lozano. Laura and Dad suddenly appear at the entrance and begin to walk slowly down the aisle to the strains of the "Wedding March." I scrutinize Dad's face, the quiet impassiveness, the smooth olive-tinted skin, the bare hint of a smile in one corner of his mouth, and it strikes me. We are like him. I turn around and the faces of my relatives blur behind me. We sit erect, spines straight, faces expressionless. Like the giant stone heads of the Mayans. Holding family knowledge

tight in our hearts. Always proud, always withhold-
ing. The faces of my childhood. Is my face the same?

The reception is held at the Elks Lodge in
Fullerton, which sits on a bluff overlooking a small
valley. The sun sinks as I drive up the narrow wind-
ing road. A breeze carries the scent of eucalyptus
mixed with the spiciness of simmering Mexican
food—oregano, chile, rice and the deep rich smell of
mole.

I enter the lodge and quickly grab a glass of
champagne. I'm early, so I choose a seat in the corner, away from the food and music and away from
the family. Aunts, uncles and cousins start to pour
in. Mom arrives with Rita's family and gracefully
moves from group to group, laughing and socializ-
ing. Mom had always wanted her girls to be more
like her, comfortable in a crowd and the life of a
party, but we turned out more like Dad. Seems like
we have more in common with the stone faces than
just looks. But Mom's frustration with her daughters' lack of social graces is greatest with me. I tend
to clam up if more than three people are present,
and this drives her crazy. As I drain my champagne
glass, I see her glance over and give me the "What
are you doing?" look. I sigh and slowly move out of
my corner and into the crowd.

"Aren't you going to even say hello to your relatives?" she asks.

"I don't think they remember me."

"Oh, they remember you. You're the one who locked herself in the bedroom whenever they came over," she says accusingly.

I sigh again in protest.

And I get her "I can't believe you" look. Tía Tomasa joins the group and I give her a hug. For me it's the same question, "How's college?" Fine, I always answer.

Children of all ages run wild as the mariachi band tunes up. The ushers and bridesmaids zigzag in slowly from their picture-taking, having had a head start on the champagne drinking.

I wander by the food table, admiring what my tías and Mom have produced. The tables are laden with plates of shredded *barbacoa*, *tortas*, beans, *chiles rellenos*, *tamales*, *mole*, *salsa* and homemade flour tortillas. Women from both sides of the family have been cooking for days. During the days of prep, Mom complained, half-jokingly, and threatened the rest of us with catered wedding fare: thin slices of ham, pale overcooked vegetables, hard rolls and cheap booze. I watch Rita balance four plates with her two daughters at her side.

"Can I help you?" I offer.

"Yeah, thanks," she says, handing me two of the plates.

"So it was nice, huh, the wedding?"

"Yeah. I knew Dad wouldn't be on time. But what did she expect? At least he showed up."

"So where's Arthur?"

"He's getting us drinks."

"How are you guys doing?"

"Okay."

Rita and Arthur have been having problems, but getting her to talk about them is close to impossible. She's even more stubborn now than as a kid. Rita escaped from the family by running away and marrying Arthur at age seventeen. I think she regrets getting married so young. And it doesn't help that Arthur is insane. He's the kind of guy who enjoys playing chicken on the road and who'll spend a whole paycheck on a stereo system. For a while Arthur had everyone believing he was a professional racecar driver and had qualified for the Indy 500.

Rita and I sit down to eat at a table filled with cousins we haven't seen in years. Everyone close to my age is married, except for my cousin William, who Mom tells me is gay. Petunia, who is my age and is my favorite cousin, is a Latina mother's dream: cute, petite and with a razor-sharp tongue. She recently married, and we make small talk, but find we don't have much in common. Petunia and I had a game in childhood where each time we saw each other, we would immediately resume our game of continuous tag, each of us remembering who had been "it" last. I resist an urge to slap her arm and run out of the hall.

The side door opens and I see Dad enter. He's grinning and he looks happy. As happy as he can be in a crowd. He joins his brothers standing in a group of men at the bar. Mom sees him come in also, and I watch her leave the table she's at, walk to the serving table, fill a plate full of food and head towards the men. My Dad takes the plate of food and kisses her on the cheek. I am confused. For years, whenever I've talked to my mother all she's ever done is complain about him. And now this. I'm amazed and a little angry. I want them to still be angry at each other, because it's how it has always been and because I am still angry. I watch them laugh and talk, and in my head I hear my father's question, "¿Carmen, *por qué te quiero tanto*?"

"Emily. Emily!" shouts Rita.

I look in the direction of her voice and realize I've been drifting. The smell of burning leaves, dusty streets and the crowing of a rooster.

"What?" I answer. I see that I am standing alone on the dance floor.

"What are you doing?" She motions from a nearby table. "What's wrong with you?"

I join her back at the table as the introduction to the next song begins.

"Oh no," she groans.

"Now what?" I ask, then realize what the groaning is about. The song. The strains of an all too familiar romantic ballad start up. One of my parents' favorites. The horns sensuously rise, violins joining in. A sprinkling of older couples take to the floor. It's as if on cue, the heartbeats quicken, memories flash and tears prepare to flow. I still don't understand my response to this music I once hated so much. I watch my Tía Clara and Tío Vicente gracefully move to the floor and feel my eyes brimming. I don't know if I'm sad over my parents' lost love or my own sense of being lost. I get up and slice through the crowd towards the bathroom. As I pass people, it's as if a switch has been turned on, as if the music has dissolved the iciness, the facades, the guards protecting these people from each other and the outside world. All around the room bodies relax, shoulders drop, hands caress and smiles appear. The room is filled with talkative, animated people. As I approach the rear of the lodge, Laura and Mike enter. I turn and watch their entrance. The reception has officially begun.

I see my father take my mother's hand and smoothly lead her to the dance floor. His left arm draws her close to him and his right arm wraps around her forearm and wrist. They clasp hands tightly. As I watch them dance, I recall the many long nights of partying and dancing held in my parents' living room and how at times, the times I remember most vividly, the evenings ended in sadness and anger, but how many more times the evenings were joyous and magical with dancing going on until the early morning, and how I would fall asleep to the humming of my aunts' and uncles' voices and the strains of the romantic ballads they loved. To my parents those evenings represented a few precious hours of release from the grind of their everyday lives—from the smell and noise of the factories, the constant demands of oh-so-many children and the pervasive, ghostly feeling of being a foreigner in your own land. Whatever mistakes my parents made and whatever flaws they may have, their fondness for each other remains. Regardless of how their children feel. There is nothing to be afraid of here.

The singer's deep, resonant voice permeates the room, and Rita and I look at each other and then watch as Laura and Mike join our parents in the dance. The yelping punctuates the powerful emotions of the song, and the whole room joins in the refrain:

y me muero por volver...
(And I'm dying to return...)

Y volver, volver, volver
(And return, return, return)

a tus brazos otra vez
(To your arms once again)

llegaré hasta donde estés
(I'll get to where you are)

yo sé perder, yo sé perder,
(I know how to lose, I know how to lose)

quiero volver, volver, volver...
(I want to return, return, return...)

Emily:
El Día de las Madres
Mother's Day

It is Mother's Day and Rita, Laura and I are taking Mom out to brunch. I invite Tía Mercy, who, after thirty-eight years of marriage is going through a divorce. She seems lonely and sad. Tía's two sons, Hector, thirty-six, and Rubén, thirty-four, are not around. I don't ask where they are, because for most of their adult lives they have been in and out of prison. I've heard talk of possession, burglary and attempted murder. I think it's mostly about drugs. It's hard to believe my two closest cousins are living their lives in jail. I still see Rubén, who is my age, in his First Communion clothes: short and shiny-faced with his ears sticking out and his front teeth missing. I look at old family pictures and try to see their present lives in their young faces. I see nothing.

Mom and I drive together to pick up Tía Mercy. With her settlement money she has moved to a mobile home in a trailer park which, ironically, sits on the same hill where El Campo Colorado was located. I want to ask her if she realizes this, but I can't, because I'm afraid what her reaction will be. I bring her a bouquet of flowers. She starts to cry. I look at my mother, but she looks uncomfortable, and so we both say nothing. Tía thanks me, wipes her tears and we pile into my Toyota.

At the restaurant we order the Mother's Day Champagne Brunch. As we eat overdone omelettes, the conversation is about jobs, husbands and children. Rita talks about her oldest child, Rachelle, who is now making college plans. Laura has just had her second baby. Gloria, who lives in San Diego with her husband and three daughters, is not present. All this talk about babies and children makes me feel out of place, like I always felt as a child. Maybe my sisters were right: maybe I was adopted.

I look over at Tía and she is quiet. She picks at her omelette. I remember how distraught Mom had been when her own marriage broke up, so distraught that her nervous breakdown lasted two years. And now fifteen years later, it is happening to her little sister. Divorce, family breakups and children in jail are a reality that my mother's Latina generation had been completely unprepared for.

After brunch we drive to the Brea Mall. My mother and Tía, although they will accept gifts purchased from pricey mall stores, will never buy anything from them.

"You pay too much money for the clothes here. They have better prices at Mervyn's."

They sit in the center of the mall and quietly wait for us to finish our shopping.

My sisters go home, and my mother and I drive Tía Mercy back to her house. She invites us in and, as she's serving coffee, Hector's name comes up.

"He's back in jail, you know?" she asks me, knowing that of course I do know.

I answer no, no I didn't know.

"I don't know what it is this time. I think it's drugs, but I don't ask anymore. I don't want to know," she adds.

I look at my mother.

"*Ay*, Mercy, when they get out, don't take them back in. You take care of them, cook, clean, give them money and they only use you. Kick them out," my mother says, her voice rising.

"Yeah, I should," Tía answers, but her heart is not in it. Neither my mother nor I believe she will do it. Both my mother and Tía could never say no to their children if their lives depended on it.

"Do you like your new home?" I ask her. The mobile home is comfortable and spacious.

"It's okay," she answers, "but it gets very cold."

She is quiet for a moment. "Emily," she says.

I look at her. "Yes?"

"Do you ever get lonely?"

"Umm, yeah, I do," I answer casually, trying not to reveal how desperately alone I sometimes feel.

"When you moved out by yourself, how long did it take you to get used to being alone?" she quietly asks.

I pause. "Not very long. You get used to it…. It takes some time but you get used to it…. But I'm sure it's not going to take you very long…."

"Oh," she replies.

My mother switches topics, and I sit there feeling like a liar. There's a part of me that will never get used to living alone. I've lived alone now for years, and although I treasure my chosen solitude, there's still something about Sunday sunsets and autumn mornings that make me melancholy.

We chat, finish our coffee and then say our goodbyes. I drive Mom back to Rita's house, where she now lives. As I head back into Los Angeles, I remember the crowded colorful holidays spent at my *tía's* house in El Campo Colorado and how many times her home was a refuge from the angry silences of my parents. Taking the Melrose exit off the 101, I pass through the bustling Thai and Latino neighborhoods before finally reaching the more sedate West Hollywood district. I park, enter my dark apartment and listen to the answering machine. No messages. I feel sad. Sad because I can't give my *tía* back that same feeling of safety she gave to me many times during my childhood. Sad because she may never become accustomed to an aloneness she never wanted. And sad because it is Sunday and the sun is slowly setting.

The heavy August air, thick with dust and smog, hangs like a yellowed tapestry over the low hills of El Campo Colorado. Family business brings me to Orange County, and as always I'm drawn to the camp. Parking my car on Buena Vista, I climb up to the railroad tracks bordering the barrio. The wooden camphouses are long-gone, as are El Veracruzano and the other small camp businesses. All that remain are the barrio homes, painted different colors, but still kept immaculately clean and with the same rose and cactus gardens carefully tended.

Twenty-five years have passed since any family members have lived here. Dad's brothers and sisters have long since left the camp to more promising neighborhoods. The shifting job market and the not-so-gentle decline of the city and the county, combined with the American-instilled desire to live apart from parents, have scattered the children and grandchildren of the Red Camp I knew.

Walking through the narrow streets, I receive suspicious sidelong glances. They know I don't belong here. Mom and my sisters won't come to the camp anymore. They say they don't know the people and there are too many foreigners. They're talking about the illegals, the immigrants from Central America and Mexico who have been moving in slowly throughout the years, drawn by the familiar atmosphere and the service-job economy of Orange County. This is now their home.

I ask myself why I keep returning here, to a place that no longer exists. Maybe it's some insane desire to make peace with the past, to make things right. Or maybe it's an attempt to confront fears I ran away from the first time around. Or maybe it's just a simple desire to be here again. To smell the cool, earthy night air, to feel the hurried rush of an evening freight train or to hear the echo of children laughing as they play late into the darkening night.